Super Special #2

Best in Class

Ahoy, mateys!

Set sail for a brand-new
adventure with the

PUPPY 🏴‍☠️ PIRATES

PUPPY PIRATES

Super Special #2

Best in Class

by Erin Soderberg
illustrations by Russ Cox

A STEPPING STONE BOOK™
Random House 🏠 New York

For all the amazing trainers and
caregivers at the Animal Humane
Society, who helped teach my pup
Wally how to make new friends
and perform a few tricks
—E.S.

Text copyright © 2017 by Erin Soderberg Downing and Robin Wasserman
Cover art copyright © 2017 by Luz Tapia
Interior illustrations copyright © 2017 by Russ Cox

Visit us on the Web!
randomhousekids.com
SteppingStonesBooks.com

Educators and librarians, for a variety of teaching tools, visit us at
RHTeachersLibrarians.com

Library of Congress Cataloging-in-Publication Data is available upon request.

ISBN 978-1-5247-1328-7 (trade) — ISBN 978-1-5247-1329-4 (lib. bdg.) —
ISBN 978-1-5247-1330-0 (ebook)

Printed in the United States of America
10 9 8 7 6 5 4 3 2 1
First Edition

This book has been officially leveled by using the F&P Text Level Gradient™
Leveling System.

CONTENTS

Captain Wally

Salty waves splashed against the side of a small wooden boat, rocking it to and fro. A sweet and cuddly golden retriever pup called Wally put his front paws on one side of the dinghy. Looking toward shore, he barked, "Land ho!"

Wally's best mate, a human boy named Henry, pulled two sturdy oars through the ocean water. The dinghy was loaded down with puppy pirates. "Land ho, mates!" Henry guided the boat toward a pier, where the pups would tie up for the day.

After many weeks searching for treasure and adventure at sea, the *Salty Bone* was running low on supplies. So Captain Red Beard had steered the puppy pirate ship toward a seaside town. The ship's crew was looking forward to a day of fun on solid ground.

"What should we do on our shore leave?" Henry asked.

"Explore!" Wally barked happily. "Play fetch! Chase!" Wally's legs were already wiggling with excitement. He could practically feel the dirt beneath his paws. Shore leave meant new smells for sniffing, soft grass for rolling, and miles and miles of dry land for fetching—with no need to worry about balls or sticks flying over the ship's rail and into the ocean!

Just as the dinghy bumped against the wooden dock, something furry whizzed over Wally's head. It missed him by inches.

Plunk!

The wooden dock shook as a chubby pug plopped onto the pier. The small, wrinkled pup slowly got up on all four paws and spun in a dizzy circle. "Blimey," she said. "Not me best landing."

"Piggly!" Wally yipped. He scrambled onto the dock to check on his prank-loving crewmate. Piggly and her twin sister, Puggly, were always getting into some kind of trouble. "Are you okay?"

"Aye," Piggly said, shaking herself off. "Me and Puggly's cannon launch has some extra *oomph* this morning. I made it from ship to shore in *four* seconds flat." Piggly grinned, flashing her gold tooth at Wally. "I was planning to catch a ride to shore in a dinghy, but there wasn't any room left for me."

Wally looked out to sea. A line of dinghies bobbed through the water, carrying puppy pirates and empty food crates from the *Salty Bone* to shore. "No room?" Wally asked. There was usually plenty of space for everyone in the ship's small cargo boats.

"No sirree," Piggly said joyfully. "Puggly

kicked me out of her boat so they could fit a trunk full o' fancy pirate costumes."

Wally cocked his head and asked, "Why?"

Before Piggly could answer, all the other dinghies arrived at the pier. Dozens of pups tumbled and wrestled and climbed out of the boats, racing down the docks. Soon only Wally, Henry, the pugs, and two other pups named Millie and Stink were left on the pier. Henry helped Puggly drag the big trunk filled with pirate outfits up onto the wooden planks.

Wally nosed the trunk open and looked inside. It was stuffed full of capes and hats and scarves and vests. Henry reached in and grabbed an old leather vest. He slid it over Wally's fluffy golden fur and laughed. "Hey, mate, what's with all the old clothes?" Henry asked.

Stink leaned forward. "Some of us overheard Captain Red Beard talking this morning," the little pup said in his scratchy voice. "There's a new pup joining our crew today. We wanted to give the furry lass a grand puppy pirate *ahoy*! Millie and I, we know what it's like to be new."

Millie bobbed her big, shaggy head and said, "Aye. We wrote a song to welcome our new crewmate."

Together, Millie and Stink howled out,

"We are the Weirdos!
We once were new
We are the Weirdos!
We welcome you!"

For many years, Millie and Stink had lived alone on an old, broken-down pirate ship. The two pups—who called themselves the Weirdos—had entertained each other by singing and dancing and turning their ship into a ghost ship. Wally was glad he had convinced the pair to join the *Salty Bone* crew. They were both a lot of fun to have on board!

"And Puggly and I," Piggly said quickly, "well, Captain Red Beard asked us to, uh, help greet our new recruit." She sneezed and snorted. It almost sounded like she was trying to hold back a laugh.

"Yeah!" Puggly giggled. She leaped into the trunk of costumes. "This is me treasure chest full of pirate finery. Wally, don't you want to get all dressed up and help us give the new pup a proper pirate welcome?"

Wally rubbed his nose with a paw. He wondered if the pugs were planning some sort of prank. Piggly and Puggly were very good at making mischief. Wally didn't like to disobey the captain's orders. And welcoming a new pup sounded like a pretty nice thing to do. "Aye, aye!" Wally barked.

Wally sat patiently while the four pups went to work dressing him and Henry in elaborate pirate costumes—eye patches, bandannas, feathered hats, leather vests, and ripped trousers.

Wally felt a little goofy. Usually, his pirate bandanna was enough to make him feel like a proper pirate.

"I look silly," Henry announced when he was all dressed.

Puggly shook her head and giggled. "You look pug-glorious!"

"And shiver me timbers, there's the new lass now," announced Millie. She lifted one of her huge, shaggy paws and pointed down the pier.

A dirt-colored Labrador retriever puppy was bounding toward them. The roly-poly pup yipped to get their attention, her tail wagging back and forth like a sausage on a stick. "Ahoy," the little pup said with a goofy grin. "I'm here to join the puppy pirate crew."

Wally stepped forward to introduce himself and his mates. But before he could say anything, Piggly barked, "Welcome to the *Salty Bone*! I'm Piggly, and this is my sister, Puggly."

Puggly cleared her throat and nosed Wally forward. "And *this* is your new boss, Captain Wally."

Wally's tongue froze. *Captain Wally?*

The New Pup

Wally spun around and stared helplessly at the pugs. *Captain Wally?* What was *that* all about? Then it hit him. This *was* another pug prank. They were playing a trick on the new pup by telling her that *Wally* was the captain of the *Salty Bone*!

Millie and Stink couldn't sing their song because they were both giggling too hard. And they were right to laugh. It *was* funny ... because it was ridiculous! *Who would ever believe I'm the captain?* Wally wondered. He didn't know the first thing about being a captain. He was just a cabin pup. He didn't want to spoil his friends' fun, but what was he supposed to do now?

"Ahoy, Captain Wally," said the new pup, her tongue lolling merrily out of her mouth.

Piggly snickered. "Go on," she told Wally, nosing him forward. "Why don't you give our new mate here a nice puppy pirate welcome . . . *Captain*?"

"Yo ho haroo!" Wally barked back. Then he cringed. He didn't sound or look anything like a puppy pirate captain. He sounded and looked silly.

Wally tried to imagine how Captain Red Beard would act. The gruff terrier loved hearing himself talk—and he sometimes said things that didn't make a lot of sense. So Wally said all the pirate words he could think of. "Blimey, ya little landlubber," Wally barked, adding a low growl to his voice. "Scalawags on the poop deck, searching for booty. Land ho!"

Puggly exploded in laughter. "Well said, Captain Wally!"

Wally tried to stand tall and proud, but his left ear flopped down, the way it sometimes did.

He felt smaller and more out of place than the day he had joined the puppy pirate crew. He made a terrible captain!

"What's your name, lass?" asked Piggly.

The new pup scratched her ear. "Name? I've only ever been called number three. I was the third pup born in my litter," she said.

"That's your name?" Stink said. "Number three?"

"That's not a name," said Millie. "We need to come up with somethin' better than that!"

"Okay!" panted the little Lab. Her whole body shook as her tail swished back and forth across the planks of the pier. "What is it?"

"How about Merry?" said Millie. "*M* names are the best, and you seem like a happy pup."

"Not Merry," argued Stink. "What about Sausage? Her tail looks like a sausage."

Wally made a face. "Sausage? That's not a good name. Someone might try to eat her."

"Wiggly?" Piggly suggested.

"Giggly?" Puggly laughed.

"I think we should get to know you first," said Wally, trying to think like a captain. "Find a name that suits you. In the meantime, we'll just call you the new pup."

"Aye, aye, Captain!" said the new pup. "Whatever you say, sir."

"That's a mighty fine idea"—Piggly giggled—"*Captain* Wally."

Wally sighed.

"Piggly and I can tell you everything you need to know about the pirate's life," Puggly said, nudging the new pup. "You're joining the mightiest ship on the sea."

"Aye," agreed Millie and Stink.

"Will we dig for treasure?" asked the new pup.

"*Will* we?" barked Puggly. "Our crew fought terrible beasties to dig up Growlin' Grace's treasure on Boneyard Island! And we uncovered even more treasure on Millie and Stink's ghost ship."

"You did?" said the new pup, her eyes wide. "Was it scary?"

"Maybe for another pirate crew," Puggly said. "But not for the pups on the *Salty Bone*." The two pugs trotted in circles around the new pup, entertaining her with stories of the crew's greatest adventures.

"Nothing we faced on Boneyard Island was nearly as scary as our crew's battle with the mighty Sea Slug," growled Piggly. "The Sea Slug lashed and thrashed and whipped her tentacles out of the sea. But we fought and lived to tell the tale."

The new pup whimpered.

"And those furball kitten pirates on the *Nine Lives* . . . ," Puggly began.

". . . are terrified of our crew," Piggly continued. "We've shredded their whiskers more times than you can even count!"

"All thanks to Captain Wally," said Puggly. Piggly giggled. "All thanks to Captain Wally."

"*Arrrf!* What's this?" barked a rough voice behind them. "Captain *Who*? What is the meaning of this?"

Wally and his mates spun around—and came face to face with the *real* puppy pirate captain. And Captain Red Beard did *not* look amused.

Wally ducked his head under his giant pirate hat. He tried to burrow inside the silly leather vest. He closed the eye that wasn't covered up with an eye patch. Because the angry look on Captain Red Beard's face? It was scarier than *anything* Wally had seen in all his puppy pirate adventures!

Puppy School

Captain Red Beard glared at the pugs. He growled at Millie and Stink. But he saved his angriest look for Wally. "I *said*, what is the meaning of this? And *what* in the name of Growlin' Grace are you wearing, little Walty?"

Piggly chewed on her back leg. Puggly sneezed, then sneezed, and sneezed again. Millie and Stink sang their song to try to distract the captain. Meanwhile, Wally cowered behind Henry's legs, thinking quickly. He needed an answer that wouldn't get them all in trouble.

"Uh," Wally said, poking his nose through Henry's legs. He tried to wriggle out of his ridiculous costume. But no matter how hard he tugged at the silly clothes, they wouldn't come off. Henry seemed to be having the same problem. The boy's hat had slipped down over his face and was now stuck. Wally's voice was shaking when he whimpered, "Sorry, Captain. W-w-we—"

The new pup looked from Wally to Captain Red Beard to the pugs. "Captain . . . ?" She looked confused. But then her face brightened when she realized what was going on. The new pup bounced toward the captain and said, "Ahoy, sir! *You* must be the captain. I am your new recruit. My new crewmates were just telling me about life on the *Salty Bone*."

Luckily, it seemed their new mate was the kind of pup who believed there were only two types of dogs in the world: friends, and friends she hadn't met yet! She didn't seem to be angry at all.

"New recruit?" Captain Red Beard growled. "What does that mean?"

The ship's first mate, Curly, cleared her throat. "Captain, we are picking up a new sailor today, remember? The pup whose grandpa used to sail with Old Salt?"

"Of course I remember!" Captain Red Beard barked quickly. "That's you?"

"Aye, aye," the new pup barked.

"Old Salt's former crew always sends along the best new sailors," Red Beard said gruffly. He lifted a paw and scratched at his scruffy, reddish beard. "I hope *you* are one of the best. What's your name?"

The new pup looked at Wally. She said, "I don't have one yet. You can just call me New Pup for now."

"New Pup it is," Red Beard began. "So tell me, New Pup. What do you know about being a pirate?"

Wally breathed a sigh of relief. Maybe Red Beard had forgotten all about the Captain Wally business!

"I don't know anything," the new pup said proudly. "But I am ready for pirate school!"

Captain Red Beard cocked his head. "Pirate school? Now what kind of hoodly-toodly nonsense are you talkin' about?"

"When puppies need to learn how to do something, they go to puppy school," the new pup said. She dug into a small sack of supplies and pulled out an apple-shaped treat. "I even brought a little gift for my first day of pirate school." She placed the meaty treat on the pier, looked around, and asked, "Which one of you is my teacher?"

"A present?" Captain Red Beard said, sniffing the treat.

Piggly scampered forward and grabbed the treat in her teeth. "I'll hold on to that for you," she said. "Keep it nice and safe . . ." In a quiet voice, she added, ". . . in my belly."

Wally was confused. After all his time on the *Salty Bone*, he thought he had figured out everything he needed to know about being a pirate. But no one had ever said anything about *school*. Then Wally noticed he wasn't the only pup who looked puzzled. In fact, none of the puppy pirates seemed to know what the new pup was talking about!

"School is where all my littermates went when it was time to leave home," the new pup said. "There were six of us. Two of my little sisters went to school to learn to be search and rescue dogs. My brother is being trained to be a farm helper. My big sister is practicing to be a show dog. The runt of our litter grew big and strong enough that she went to a special school for hunting dogs!"

Wally remembered his first days on the *Salty Bone*. Back then, he didn't know *anything* about being a pirate. He and Henry had to figure it out on the job. If he had failed, he would have been forced to walk the plank! Having someone teach him everything he needed to know? That sounded like much more fun.

"No one told *us* about pirate school," Millie barked, looking confused. "Were we supposed to go to school when we joined the crew?"

Stink sighed. "Pirate school sounds fun." He nudged Millie and whispered in her ear, "But what *is* pirate school?"

Curly laughed. "You didn't go to pirate school because pirates learn by doing! You learn how to be a pirate by being a pirate."

The new pup hung her head. Her big eyes looked sad when she asked, "So . . . I don't get to go to school?"

"You heard the first mate," Captain Red Beard said. "Pirates don't do school."

"So no ribbons?" asked the new recruit. "No medals or certificates?"

"Medals?" barked Captain Red Beard. His ears pricked up. "Ribbons? What kind of ribbons?"

Puggly yelped. She *always* liked the sound of ribbons.

"At the end of puppy school, the teacher names one of the students Best in Class. And that pup gets a fancy medal! The other puppies get special certificates to show everything they have learned." The new pup got so excited talking about puppy school that the whole back half of her body was wiggling.

"Hmmm," Captain Red Beard said. "What *color* are these medals? Gold?" Everyone knew how much the captain liked gold.

"I don't know," said the new pup. "But I was going to work extra hard to win one at puppy pirate school." She sat up proudly on her haunches. "My grand-paw told me you only want the best puppy pirates on your crew. I was ready to learn everything I could so I can be the best!"

"This new pup has a point!" Captain Red Beard barked. "How am I supposed to have the best pirate ship in all the seven seas if I don't send me crew to pirate school?" He stomped his paw. "It's decided. We must send our whole crew to puppy pirate school. Then they can *all* learn how to be the best—and get ribbons to prove it."

"Uh, Captain, where will we find a pirate school?" Curly asked. "I've never heard of one."

"We'll *make* one," Captain Red Beard boomed. Once he bit down on an idea, he never let go. "New Pup, tell me everything you know about school."

There was a long silence. The new pup looked down. "Well . . . I've never actually been to school," she finally said.

The captain howled, "How are we supposed to start a school if we don't know anything about it?"

Wally wasn't sure. No one was. None of them had been to school.

Then, suddenly, Curly leaped forward. "You said your town has a school for puppies to learn things?" she asked the new pup. Wally could tell Curly had thought of something. The tiny white poodle was one of the smartest pups Wally had ever met, and she always had great ideas.

"Not pirate kinds of things," the new pup said.

"But it's a *school*," Curly said. "Puppies go there to learn *something*?"

The new pup shrugged. "I guess."

Curly whispered to Captain Red Beard. A moment later, the captain's tail began to wag. "I just had a brilliant idea!" he barked. "Are you pups ready for a mission?"

Wally and his mates looked at each other eagerly. They nodded. Puppy pirates were always ready for a mission.

"Good!" Captain Red Beard barked. "Because today you are going to puppy school!"

Miss Manners

This was the plan: Wally, Henry, the pugs, and the new pup would sneak into the town's puppy school. They would figure out what *school* was. They would report back to the captain. Then they could make their very own pirate school on board the *Salty Bone.*

"This will be the easiest mission we've ever gone on," Piggly bragged.

Puggly thought so, too. But she was worried about leaving all her costumes behind.

"We'll protect your treasure for you," Stink offered. Wally wasn't surprised. The Weirdos loved costumes almost as much as the captain loved gold.

"We can get dressed up fancy and put on a pirate play for all the landlubbers!" Millie woofed.

"Aye, aye, *arooo*!" Stink agreed.

As soon as Wally and Henry wriggled out of their pirate costumes, the group set off on their special mission. When they arrived at puppy school, the first thing Wally noticed was how big the school building was—larger, even, than the *Salty Bone*.

"Hey, look! Puppy Academy," Henry read, staring up at big letters painted on the side of the building. "In case you were wondering, *academy* is a fancy word for school. Let's check it out!"

The pugs, Wally, and Henry all followed the new pup through the school's front door. There were so many dogs inside that no one gave the puppy pirates a second look. "It was even easier to get into school than I thought it would be," Piggly said.

"Aye," agreed Puggly. "No guards! No booby traps! No need to sneak in! So far, puppy school is a piece of cake." Inside the building, the huge open space had been broken up into many smaller rooms. It looked like each room was used for a different kind of class.

"This is a basic skills and obedience training class," Henry said, pointing to a nearby sign. "In case you were wondering, *obedience* means 'following directions.' Should we go in?"

The four pups and Henry nosed around the edge of the door. Inside, there was a big open space with a grass-covered floor. Grass *inside*? Wally had never seen anything so odd!

He sniffed eagerly. It didn't smell like the outdoors. It smelled like . . . plastic.

A class of puppies sat in the center of the room, practicing skills like "stay," "shake," "down," and "leave it."

Wally couldn't believe all the dogs were able to stay so still and so quiet. Because the moment *he* walked into the room, a flurry of new scents overwhelmed him. Fresh treats to taste! New dogs to sniff! The marks of hundreds of different dogs on the walls and floors! It was a scent explosion. Wally didn't know what to smell first. He bounced back and forth across the room, shoving his nose into everything he could find.

The pugs were having the same problem. They had been stuck on their ship for too long. They raced in circles, noses in the air, sniffing all the wonderful smells.

The sudden commotion excited all the other puppies in the arena. Before long, the room was filled with barking and running dogs—and no one was sitting anymore.

Henry chased after his crewmates. He yelled, "Hey, mates. In case you were wondering, you aren't supposed to run around at school!" Henry tried to catch Wally and the pugs. But Wally was too quick, and the pugs too clever, to get caught. "This is not the way obedience training works."

Wally stopped sniffing long enough to wonder if Henry knew how school *did* work. He certainly knew everything there was to know about being a pirate, so maybe he was a *school* expert, too. But before he could ask him, a tiny poodle pup ran by and Wally got distracted again.

When all the dogs had finally calmed down, class was able to get under way.

Wally watched the dogs in the ring practice their tricks. They seemed very proud of themselves. But he wasn't impressed. The skills these puppies were learning sounded like basic stuff to him! Wally thought it was rather boring to teach this stuff in school.

"Sit" was a very simple thing to understand. Rump on the ground, and that was that.

And who needed to be *told* to shake? Shaking when you met someone new was just good manners.

Of course, every great puppy pirate knew that if your captain told you to stay, you *stayed*—or paid the consequences.

How silly was it to learn about lying down in school? Lying down was something every dog knew very well. If you felt tired, it was time to lie down!

Maybe puppy pirates were smarter than all other types of dogs.

"This is like a manners class," Henry explained after they had watched for a while. He gave Piggly a sly look and said, "You could probably learn something here, Miss Manners."

Piggly snorted at him and backed out the door. The other pups followed her to the next classroom, where dogs were learning search and rescue skills. This class was much more interesting to watch. And puppy pirates knew a thing or two about search and rescue. After all, that was a pirate's job: search for treasure, then rescue it!

The teacher was showing the pups in class how to sniff out scents and follow a trail. She covered a special toy in ham fat, then tossed the toy across the room for someone to fetch. When the student brought it back, he got a treat.

"Blimey!" Piggly said after watching the lesson

for a minute. "In this class, you get a treat just for playing fetch!"

The little brown Lab started fidgeting. "Fetch," she whispered. "I want to fetch!"

Wally knew how the new pup felt. He was a retriever, just like her. They were *born* to fetch. Just seeing the toy fly across the room, Wally felt all itchy and twitchy. He wanted to race after it! But he knew better. "We're only here to watch," he reminded the new pup. "We have to—"

It was too late. The little Lab burst into the room and went racing for the toy. None of the other students wanted to lose their turn … so they went racing for it, too! Soon the well-behaved class had turned into a wild pack of puppies, each pup trying to fetch the same toy.

"Out!" the teacher barked sharply.

Everyone knew exactly who she was talking to. The little Lab hung her head and trotted out of the classroom. The rest of the puppy pirates followed her.

"It's okay," Wally told the new pup. "Look, there's another class right here."

"Show dog training," Henry announced, after reading the sign on the door. The group walked inside to get a closer look. Dozens of dogs stood in a neat circle around the outside of the room. All the dogs looked like they had taken a bath that very day. Some pups had little bows in their fur, like Puggly often wore, and others had haircuts that must have taken hours! The strangest thing was that the class was almost completely silent, and no one was moving.

Wally and the others waited for something to happen. But the dogs just kept standing there.

And standing there.

Finally, after what felt like a hundred hours, the lead dog stepped into the center of the ring.

He trotted slowly around the room in a perfect circle. One by one, each of the students took a turn doing the same thing. It was the most boring thing the puppy pirates had ever seen.

Puggly was the most bored. She yawned. Then she started sniffing around the edges of the classroom. She nosed open a box filled with ribbons. "Loot!" she woofed. The other puppy pirates surrounded her. Puggly hopped inside the box and buried herself under hundreds of different-colored ribbons.

Henry rustled around at the bottom of the box. He pulled out a big gold medal. He studied the front of the medal. "Best in Class," he said, reading the words. He draped the medal over his own chest and laughed. "Look, mates! I won Best in Class at puppy school."

Once Puggly had played inside the box of ribbons for a while, she continued her search for fun. She tipped over a box of toys, spilled a pail of treats, and then nosed open a chest filled with tiny dog tutus. "Lookie here, Piggly!" she whispered. "This is the kind of show dog *I* like to watch!" She whipped off her cape and booties and wiggled into one of the frilly skirts. She balanced on her hind legs, jumped in circles, and giggled as the tutu fanned out around her smushy belly. "Hey, show dogs!" she barked. "It's showtime!"

A Giant Treasure Map

Puggly spun and wiggled. She jumped and leaped across the center of the circle. All the dogs with their fancy bows and haircuts sniffed and stared. The teacher yelled, "You there! This is *not* appropriate."

But Piggly was singing a pirate shanty so loudly that Puggly couldn't hear the teacher. Puggly continued to spin while Piggly sang, and Wally howled along. It wasn't long before the puppy pirates were chased out of yet *another* classroom.

"It's called show dog class," Puggly complained, putting her cape and booties back on. "I thought they'd *want* to see my show!"

The next room had a sign that said AGILITY TRAINING. Henry patted Wally on the head and explained, "In case you were wondering, in agility training you get to jump over stuff and climb through things. You, mate, are going to be great at this class!"

The inside of this classroom was very different from the first two. Wally thought it looked like a giant treasure map you could trot around on.

"Check out this obstacle course!" Henry said, his eyes wide. "And look what you get if you make it all the way to the end!"

Along the course were dark tunnels and hanging rings, colorful hills to climb and jumps to leap over, tall poles to weave through, and narrow planks to race across. The narrow planks looked a lot like the wooden plank on the *Salty Bone*! There was a path to follow through the room, and at the end of the path was a basket full of treats! Dogs of all sizes raced from one side of the room to another, then back and forth.

Wally's legs felt itchy again.
He longed to play!

Piggly nudged Wally. "Maybe one of us should try it," she suggested. "Curly said it herself: pirates learn by doing. Should we give this class a try?"

Wally barked, "Aye!"

So Wally, Piggly, Puggly, and the new pup all lined up with the group of puppies learning agility training. Wally went first. He weaved his way around the poles, raced up and over hills, burrowed through a tunnel, and leaped through rings— including one that was on fire! Then he collected his treasure. It tasted even better than it looked.

Wally lay down—without anyone telling him to!—and breathed hard, trying to catch his breath. The new pup got to the end of the path just after Wally. Her tongue lolled out of her mouth.

Piggly and Puggly were next. Puggly's frilly cape and booties and tutu made it hard for her to jump high. So instead of going through the rings or leaping over jumps, Puggly scurried under them.

Piggly's belly was so close to the floor that it got caught on one of the rings when she tried to jump through the center. Henry had to lift her the rest of the way over. Piggly wiggled down the path as fast as she could. But the little pug was so out of breath by the time she made it to the top of the ramp that she rolled down the hill on the other side.

Then Puggly got stuck in the long tunnel. Henry had to crawl in after her and pull her out

by her front paws. "No humans in the course!"
barked the teacher.

Finally, the two pugs galloped together
toward the end of the track. Several other dogs
in the class were close at their tails. Piggly and
Puggly each dashed around the ring of fire, and
then pounced onto the basket of treats. Several

more dogs leaped through the ring moments afterward. They landed right on top of the pugs, who were scarfing down treats.

"*Oof!*" Piggly grunted through a mouthful of treats.

"Blimey," moaned Puggly.

"Puppy pile!" yipped the new pup. She raced forward and jumped onto the furry pile to play with all the other students. But none of the other pups wanted to wrestle—they all looked upset at the puppy pirates for getting in the way.

Piggly poked her head out from under another dog and blinked at Wally. She flashed her gold-toothed smile and asked, "Did ya see how good I looked out there? Think I'll win the prize for Best in Class?"

"Uh, I think it's time for us to go, mates!" Henry said. Dozens of dogs had gathered in the doorway of the classroom. They were *all* glaring at the puppy pirates.

Puggly and Piggly squeezed out from under the pile of dogs. The puppy pirates darted past the crowd of angry dogs in the doorway. They raced down the hall, past the basic skills classroom, and through the front door of the puppy school.

But as soon as they got outside, they skidded to a stop. A group of hairy sheepdogs, shepherds, and collies stood in a line, looking alert and ready. Henry chewed at his lip. "We're in trouble, mates. I think the herding class is after us!"

Herd 'Em Up

"In case you were wondering, herding dogs are very good at catching and collecting things," Henry explained in a hurry. "They go to school so they can work on farms or in fields. Their job is to keep a pack of animals together—like cows or sheep." His eyes widened. "And now I have a feeling they're going to try to herd *us*!"

A big shepherd dog barked, "Catch that pack, herders! I need to speak with these intruders."

Wally's thoughts raced. If the herding dogs were trying to keep their pack together, then the puppy pirates should do the opposite. "Scatter!" he barked.

The puppy pirates ran in different directions. The herding class split up and raced after them, barking loudly. Piggly and Puggly squirmed under a fence. Wally dashed one way, then the other, trying to fool the herding class and tire them out. The new pup yelped, "Catch me if you can!"

Henry raced toward the harbor. "Come on, mates. Let's get to the ship!"

"Follow me," the new pup barked. "I know a shortcut back to the pier." She quickly turned left into a narrow alleyway. The others chased her down a set of crumbling stairs. The excited barks of the herding dogs were not far behind.

"Hurry!" Henry yelled. "They're gaining on us!"

"I can't run much farther," Piggly huffed. Her jiggly belly bounced on the ground with each step. "Pugs weren't built for speed."

"All that dancing and hoop jumping did me in," Puggly said. "And I never thought I'd say this, but this tutu is *too much*. It's slowin' me down!"

Piggly's belly hit a step and she tripped over her own front left paw. She rolled down the last few stairs. "Avast!" she barked. "Pirate down! I repeat, we have a pirate *down*!"

Henry jumped over her. Then he swept the silly pug up into his arms. Seconds later, the group was off and running again. Piggly snuggled into Henry's chest and closed her eyes. "Aye, this is the life."

"Lucky dog!" Puggly whined.

Piggly smirked down at her sister and said, "I guess this is payback for you kickin' me out o' the dinghy this morning. *Now* who's riding in style?"

The little Lab led the puppy pirates through an open door at the back of a line of shops. "In here," she said. "We can cut through the butcher shop and sneak out the front door. The herding dogs won't dare come through here—the butcher in town is a real grump, but he likes me. Keep your heads down and don't take *anything*!"

Just inside the door, Wally jumped over a big bucket. He squirmed between two giant crates. They were in a storage room at the back of the butcher shop. It looked a lot like the room where Steak-Eye kept all the crew's food in the belly of their ship. The floor-to-ceiling shelves were stuffed with sausage links, chicken liver, and beef sticks. Wally wished they had time to stop for a snack, but the herding dogs' barks sounded closer than ever. They wouldn't fool them for long.

Besides, the new pup had warned them not to take anything. The last thing they needed was an angry butcher chasing after them, too. Wally knew they had better keep moving.

As Henry ran past the stuffed shelves, Piggly's nose caught a whiff of all the delicious food. She opened her eyes wide and tried to squirm out of Henry's arms. "This is my stop," she said.

But Henry held her tight to his chest. "Oh, no, you don't," he warned. "We are not stopping for a snack break now."

Piggly snorted in his face and growled.

Puggly snatched up a sausage in her flat snout. "Pug-glorious!" she cheered. "Look at *this* booty, Piggly," she bragged. "Yummer nummers! Mmm mmm mmm." She stood up on her hind legs and danced in happy circles with the sausage held tight between her teeth. But a few seconds later, Puggly found she was tangled up in a long meaty rope. The sausage in her mouth was connected to another, and another, and another. She had managed to snag a whole *rope* made of sausages!

Henry untangled her, muttering, "Seriously, mate?" He grunted as he swept Puggly up into his arms along with Piggly. "In case you were wondering, it takes a mighty tough pirate to carry two stinky pugs."

"Stinky!" Puggly gasped. "How dare you? I smell like sausages and the sea!"

"Are you coming?" yipped the little brown Lab. "The coast is clear."

Henry and Wally burst out of the butcher's storage room and raced through the front of the shop. The butcher dog growled at them, but calmed when the friendly little Lab called out, "Ahoy, Toby!"

"Good luck on your seafaring adventures, li'l one!" Toby called back.

Henry, Wally, and the Lab puppy burst out the shop's front door—and straight into Steak-Eye, the *Salty Bone*'s cranky cook. The little Chihuahua was loading the last of his dinner supplies on a giant cart.

"Ahoy, Steak-Eye!" Wally cried. "Where are Wayne and Otis?" The big Great Dane and his Saint Bernard pal were supposed to be helping Steak-Eye get all the food back to the ship. Food for the puppy pirate crew was heavy!

"Those lazy bums are still playin' around, I guess," growled Steak-Eye. He took the rope on one side of the cart in his tiny jaw and tried to tug it. "*Oof!*" he grunted. "Those two brutes left me here alone to carry all me own stuff."

"I've got it!" Henry shouted. "No time to explain, but we need to get back to the ship *now*." He quickly plopped the two pugs on top of

Steak-Eye's pile of food, then grabbed the rope and began to pull. Safe and comfy inside the cart, the pugs snuck samples of Steak-Eye's supplies.

Wally and the new pup dashed through the town's main street, with Henry and Steak-Eye right behind. They raced past a big open field. Wally could see the rest of the crew chasing and playing in the grass. He barked out a warning. "To the ship!" he howled. "*Arrrr-oooo!*"

Wally glanced back over his shoulder. A hundred paces behind, the herding class was drawing closer. And they weren't alone. It looked like the whole puppy school was chasing them now! Several hundred paces ahead, the sparkling sea and the *Salty Bone* were waiting.

The cart bounced wildly as it bumped and thumped toward the harbor. Piggly and Puggly stretched their bodies across the top of the food to keep it from flying into the air.

When the group reached the pier, Captain Red Beard barked, "Load up, me barkies! Let's set sail!"

All the puppy pirates jumped into dinghies, pushing crates of supplies in wherever there was space. The little boats bobbed. Some were so weighed down with pups and supplies that they were barely staying afloat. Spike, the nervous bulldog, whimpered and hid under his friend Humphrey's blanket. Millie and Stink shoved the crate of costumes into the last empty space. Wally and Henry pulled the new pup into their boat.

With just seconds to spare, the whole fleet of dinghies pushed away from the dock. The puppy school students were left shaking their paws and barking back on shore while the puppy pirates sailed out to sea.

7

School Report

"Yo ho haroo!" the new pup cheered when they were all aboard the *Salty Bone*. "Anchors aweigh!" The little Lab raced back and forth across the deck, watching as the crew prepared the ship for deep waters. She bounded past the wet and sandy anchor, up to the top of the pointy bow, then back to the stern of the ship.

In just a few minutes, she had tested out a spyglass to get a closer look at the pups on shore (but she held it backward), found her bed (after

burying herself in a few that were already taken), dug up a bandanna to wear (but the captain told her she had to earn it first), and introduced herself to every pup on the crew. Wally was impressed with her speed and jolly mood. It was going to be fun to have such a happy new friend on board.

The little pup leaped around on the deck. She raced up to Captain Red Beard and announced, "That chase through town was so fun! Is life always this *exciting* for pirates?"

"Absotootly," he said, smiling. The new
pup even put the gruff captain in a good mood.
"Now tell me, pups. What did you learn about
this thing called school? I want a full report."

Wally, Piggly, Puggly, and the new pup
lined up before their captain. Henry was helping
a few of the larger pups carry supplies down to the
belly of the boat. The rest of the crew gathered
on the deck as the group shared the details of
their day.

Wally went first. He told the captain how puppy school had many different classes with many different subjects.

"What's a subject?" the captain asked.

Wally gave him a few examples. "There is a basic skills class, where puppies learn simple things like how to sit, stay, and lie down."

"Sit!" Captain Red Beard barked. Every pup on deck sat. Captain Red Beard woofed. "Excellent. It seems me crew has mastered their basic skills. That's what I like to see!"

"We also went to a search and rescue class," the new pup said. "There, all the pups were learning how to find things that are lost."

"Sounds like the time we found Growlin' Grace's buried treasure on Boneyard Island!" Captain Red Beard boasted. "That's simple stuff."

"Or the time we found the Sea Slug in the deepest, darkest part of the ocean," added Einstein shyly. Wally winked at the scrawny pup.

The pirates never could have found the Sea Slug without Einstein's help.

Next, Piggly told the captain, "Every class has a teacher."

"And what does the teacher do?" Captain Red Beard asked.

"The teacher gets to tell the students what to do," Piggly said.

"And what not to do," Puggly added quietly.

"They lead the lesson," Wally added.

"That sounds like a job for me!" Captain Red Beard said. He loved telling other puppies what to do. "But get to the prize part of school. The new pup said there would be ribbons and medals!"

"Yes," Wally said. "When the students at puppy school do a good job with something, they get a prize." He thought about the giant obstacle course. "Most of the time, it's a treat."

"Or sometimes a medal, right?" the captain barked. "A *gold* medal?"

"We found a box full of prizes while we were at school," Puggly said, pulling a gold medal out of her tutu. She wiggled and tugged, and a bunch of ribbons spilled out onto the deck. "I think they give them out at the end of the class, but we didn't stay long enough to find out for sure."

"It's gold treasure!" Captain Red Beard cried. "So this is what you get for being the best?"

"Aye, aye, Captain," barked the new pup. She didn't tell him that wasn't how *Puggly* got her loot.

"Being the best is the *best*!" said the captain. "Three cheers for winning at school!"

The rest of the crew cheered.

Old Salt pounded his peg leg on the ship's deck to make himself heard. "Hold on," he said in his low voice. "Now I'm not so sure that is the point of school. I am not a puppy school expert, but I think the whole point of taking classes is to *learn*. Not to win ribbons and medals."

But Wally could tell the captain wasn't listening to the wise old dog. Red Beard was too busy nosing around the ribbons and the gold medal. "Listen up, me crew," he said. The pups waited while the captain scratched his chin. He chewed at his paw. Finally, he announced, "Tomorrow we will hold the first, and only, day of puppy pirate school on the *Salty Bone*. School is where you learn to be the best. So we will learn how to be the best crew in all the seven seas!"

Mast Master

Pirate school needed teachers. The captain realized he couldn't teach all the classes himself because he was too busy running the ship. But plenty of pups on the crew volunteered to help out. The *Salty Bone* was packed with puppies who were good at all kinds of pirate things. And they were eager to have a chance to teach their mates.

Once all the teachers were decided, everyone gathered on the deck for their first class at puppy pirate school: a lesson in mast climbing.

Olly the beagle was the teacher. He took his job very seriously.

"Climbing up the mast is one of the most important things to master as a member of this crew," Olly told his students. "The quicker you get to the top, the quicker you can keep lookout. And keeping lookout helps us spot enemy ships and other dangers."

"Like icebergs!" Captain Red Beard called out. He was sitting way at the back of the class. "Warm seawater like this has *lots* of icebergs. We have to keep a close lookout!"

"Uh," Olly said. Wally could tell he didn't want to argue with the captain. "Icebergs . . . or the Sea Slug, or the kitten pirate ship, or—"

From nearby, Curly interrupted, "Yes, Captain, icebergs are something we would need to worry about in the arctic seas. I'm sure you meant to say *cold* water, correct?"

"Correct-o-nino!" Captain Red Beard said, looking around to see if anyone else had noticed his mistake.

"As I was saying," Olly continued, "to be a mast master, you have to run as fast as you can. Just keep your legs moving, and you will be up to the top lickety-split." Olly ran toward the long, slim rope ladder that led up to the ship's crow's nest. Without stopping, he raced up, up, up—and within seconds he was at the top. He ran back down and said, "See? Easy."

Piggly groaned. "That does *not* look easy."

"Who wants to try first?" Olly asked.

At the back of the class, Captain Red Beard waved a green ribbon between his teeth. He said, "Whichever pup climbs fastest wins the ribbon for this class."

"Captain Red Beard *really* seems to love those ribbons," Henry said.

"Lucky for us," Wally barked. If it weren't for the ribbons, the captain might never have agreed to a pirate school. And Wally was already sure school was going to be *lots* of fun.

"Come on," Olly urged. "Who's going first?"

No one wanted to be first. Everyone was worried about being embarrassed or doing it wrong. Watching someone else go first felt much less scary. But Wally knew *someone* had to paw up or they would be standing around all day, waiting. So he volunteered. The other pups cheered him on, which made things easier.

Wally thought about the three tricks he had already discovered about climbing the mast ropes:

1. It was important to step onto the center of his paw pads. If he didn't, his claws got caught in the rope.
2. Always look *up* at the crow's nest, instead of *down* at the deck. He moved faster when he was looking at his goal.
3. Light, quick steps were a big help when moving fast.

When Olly said, *"Go,"* Wally was ready. He kept these tips in mind and raced up. He wasn't fast and he hadn't done it perfectly, but everyone cheered for him anyway.

Piggly went next, followed by Puggly. Both pugs quickly discovered their legs were too small, and their bellies too big, to make it an easy job. They got stuck in the rope, and Henry had to help them out.

"I'm scared," the new pup said quietly. She watched as Henry took his turn climbing up.

"What if I do it wrong?"

"It's okay if you do it wrong," Wally promised her. Then he told her about the three tricks that helped him get up the mast. "They might not work for you, but it's worth a try."

"Thanks, Wally," the new pup said. "I love learning new tricks." Then she took her turn—and she was faster than anyone who had gone yet!

"Good job!" Wally cheered, along with all the other students.

"Can I share your tips with my new friends?" the pup asked, panting to catch her breath.

"Of course," said Wally.

So the little Lab raced around, sharing Wally's tricks for mast climbing. By the end of class, even Piggly and Puggly were able to use Wally's tips to make it up.

"Well done, mates," said Olly. "You all did a great job."

"Who climbed the fastest?" Red Beard barked. The captain had decided not to take any of the puppy pirate classes himself. He was pretty sure he knew everything there was to know about being a pirate.

"It was a tie," Olly said. "Between the new pup, Leo, and me."

The rest of the pups in class cheered. Wally was a little sad he hadn't won, too. It would be hard to see other pups get ribbons. He wished *everyone* could win.

"Maybe next time *we* will win," Wally whispered to Henry. Then he tugged at his best mate's sleeve, pulling him toward their next class.

9

You Can't Teach an Old Dog New Tricks

After they had finished the mast-climbing lesson, the crew moved on to map reading with Einstein. This class met in the map room, which was near the captain's quarters below deck.

A German shepherd named Chumley ran the map room. The big dog kept a very close eye on Einstein all through class, making sure nothing bad happened to any of his maps. Einstein was one of the smartest pups on board the *Salty Bone,* but he was also *very* clumsy. He often lost things, or tripped over things, or got tangled up in his own tail.

Einstein began class by telling them that north was always at the top of the map, south was at the bottom, east was on the right, and west was on the left.

"Allow me to show you," said Captain Red Beard, stepping forward. Once again, he was lurking around at the back of the group, eager to take over. He reached out a paw and pointed to one edge of the map. "Repeat after me: *north.*"

All the pups said, "North."

"Uh," Einstein muttered. "You are looking at the map upside down, sir. That is actually *south.*"

"As I said, *south,*" grumbled Captain Red Beard.

The puppy pirates echoed him: "South."

Though Einstein's voice was quiet, he was very good at teaching them the parts of a map. Wally had always thought maps looked confusing, but the way Einstein explained everything made it seem so simple! Einstein showed the pups how to tell land from water, and also how to pay attention to little lines that showed the deepest parts of the sea.

Wally noticed that Old Salt was sitting quietly at the edge of the class, saying nothing.

"Everything okay, Old Salt?" he asked.

"Aye, Wally," sighed Old Salt. "But maps are not my thing, pup."

"What do you mean?" asked Wally.

"I cannot read letters," said Old Salt. "And alas, my time for learnin' is long past. You can't teach an old dog new tricks."

"You don't need to be able to read letters to read a map," said Wally. He whispered, "The *S* in south looks like a sea monster. That's how I remember where south is. If you can find the *S* for south sea monster, you know that's the bottom of the map!"

Old Salt peered over the map. His face brightened. "South sea monster. Blimey, that's a beauty of a trick."

Henry proved he had great map-reading skills during class. He kept stepping forward to point things out, acting like he was Einstein's assistant. When it came time to pick the best in the class, Henry won! The captain also promised Einstein a ribbon for being such a good teacher.

"*Arrrr-oooo!*" Wally cheered.

The strangest class of the day was captain class. This was the only class taught by Captain Red Beard. He tried to tell everyone how to run the ship, but really all he did was talk very loudly and boss people around. Each of the pups tried copying him. The ship grew noisy as everyone shouted orders at their friends.

The new pup whispered, "So I guess the most important part of being the captain is barking and taking charge?"

"Aye," Wally agreed, though he wasn't really sure. He thought about how Curly was often the pup who listened to the problem and saved the day. Or sometimes it was Old Salt.

No matter how it was done, Wally was sure he could never take control of the crew the way Captain Red Beard did.

"Remember when Piggly and Puggly told me *you* were the captain?" The new pup giggled. "You looked like such an important pirate!" Wally laughed along with her. He still couldn't believe she had fallen for the prank.

The final class of their puppy pirate school was survival training. First mate Curly was helping the crew understand what to do if something happened to their ship. The whole crew gathered around as Curly explained how important it was to leave everything behind and get to one of the dinghies right away. "You don't need your spyglass, or your maps, or your blanket, or even your brush. . . ." The crew chuckled. Curly *loved* her brush. She used it several times a day to keep her poodle fur from getting tangled. "In an emergency, you work together to get to safety. Get into a dinghy, fill it up with pups, and row away from the ship."

"Shall we try it?" barked Captain Red Beard. "Every pup, to the rescue boats! Hurry, hurry, or you'll be left behind!"

"Wait! I haven't finished my lesson," Curly barked. She raced around, trying to tell everyone to slow down and listen. "It's important to stay calm. Don't panic." But no one could hear Curly's voice over the sounds of the captain's loud orders.

Wally knew this was his last chance to win a ribbon. So he joined all the other puppies and raced toward a boat. The trouble was, everyone was trying to load into the boats at the same time. They stumbled and tumbled over each other, and soon there were more than twenty pups in Wally's dinghy.

Wally called out, "There are too many of us! We need to split up." But no one heard him over the shouting and barking.

Someone in the middle of the boat howled, "Let out the line!"

A moment later, the dinghy lurched and began to fall. "Wait!" Henry yelled. But it was too late to stop—the very full boat dropped down and plunked into the water.

Up on the main deck, Wally could see Henry shaking his head. As the overcrowded dinghy bobbed away from the *Salty Bone,* the boy threw his hands into the air and yelled, "In case you were wondering, you don't have any oars!"

10

Captain Practice

There was hardly any room to move inside the dinghy. Wally was squished between two other pups. But the boat itself was having no trouble moving. Little waves pushed the group away from the hull of the *Salty Bone,* sending the puppy pirates out toward the open sea.

"No oars!" Spike moaned, hiding his face between his paws. "There are no oars."

"We be doomed!" cried Willard the sheepdog.

"Curly never told us what to do once we got into the escape boat," groaned Piggly.

"I'm scared," whimpered the new pup.

Wally squirmed, trying to get his left front paw free. It was stuck under Wayne, the enormous Great Dane. Water sloshed against the edges of the boat, making the dinghy rock back and forth. Every time it tipped from side to side, a few pups lost their balance. This made the little boat rock even harder.

The more they rocked, the closer the edge of the boat got to the water's surface. Every time they tilted too far to one side, rippling waves rolled up and over the side of the dinghy.

Wally waited for someone to take control. That's what always happened when there was trouble on board the ship—Captain Red Beard, or Curly, or Old Salt would take charge and tell the other pups what to do. Wally

looked around. He realized that Captain Red
Beard, Curly, *and* Old Salt were looking down
at them from the main deck of the *Salty Bone*.
They couldn't help.

Henry tried throwing a rope to the puppies
in the dinghy. But the group had already floated
too far away from the ship. The rope wasn't long
enough to reach them.

Pups began to panic. Leo the black Lab suggested everyone jump out of the rescue boat and swim back toward the ship. The best swimmers in the group were quick to agree.

"But I can't swim," sobbed Spike. "And Humphrey's too little to keep his head above the waves!"

"Our boat's leaking," shrieked Puggly. She barked three times to signal danger.

Wally peered through the tangle of legs and paws and saw that there was indeed a small leak in the bottom of the boat. It was just a tiny crack, but before long their boat would be filled with water.

"We be doomed!" Willard howled again. This announcement sent Spike into a panic. He began to whimper. Other puppies started blaming each other for crowding the boat. Before long, they were all growling and howling and snapping at each other.

Wally didn't know what to do. The new pup was scared and shaking beside him. His friends were fighting with each other. The water in the bottom of the boat was getting deeper. The sky was streaked with orange and pink, getting darker by the minute. Night was coming fast.

They were all in terrible danger. Clearly, someone had to take charge. Wally had pretended to be the captain of their ship that morning on the pier—why not pretend again? He thought back to Red Beard's captain lessons. Maybe this was the perfect time to try some of the things he had learned. "Everyone, calm down!" he barked. His voice was so loud he surprised even himself. He shouted, "Fighting is doing us no good!"

The other pups quieted down. They all looked at him.

Wally took a deep breath.

The crew waited. *His* crew.

Wally had managed to take charge of the little dinghy! Speaking in a strong voice, he ordered, "Spike, sit on the leak."

"M-m-m-me?" Spike whimpered.

"Yes," Wally said. "You have the biggest back-side. If you sit right on the crack, you can help keep the water out." Spike did as he was told.

Next, Wally ordered some of the strongest swimmers to jump into the water. "If you all swim in a group behind the boat, you can push us back toward the ship with your snouts." A few big dogs jumped into the water and dog-paddled into position.

Then Wally said calmly, "Everyone else, sit still so we stop rocking the boat."

Wally wiggled his way to the front of the dinghy. He barked out orders to the swimmers, telling them which way to steer the boat. At first, it didn't seem like Wally's plan was working—but once they got moving, their little dinghy began to float in the right direction. They were getting closer to the *Salty Bone*!

"Go, Captain Wally!" barked the new pup.

"Three cheers for Captain Wally!" the rest of the pups yelled.

When the little dinghy bumped up against the side of the *Salty Bone,* Wally swelled with pride. They were going to make it—and he had helped. Maybe Wally knew a little more about being a pirate captain than he had realized!

11

Back on Board

As soon as the pups had been pulled out of the water, they took a count to make sure no one was missing. They were all safe. Henry ran over and threw his arms around Wally, happy to have his best mate back by his side.

Everyone began to celebrate. But they quickly realized they weren't out of danger yet—because Curly was *furious*.

The first mate climbed up on top of a stack of crates and growled at the crew. "That was a perfect example of what *not* to do when the ship or your crewmates are facing danger," she snapped. "Panic, chaos, and rushing are the *opposite* of staying calm and keeping order."

"But—" Spike whimpered. He glanced at Wally. Wally felt happy when he realized his mate was trying to tell Curly about how he had taken charge.

"No buts!" Curly snarled.

Puggly giggled and whispered to her sister, "One big butt helped save our fur today."

Curly took a deep breath. Then she said calmly, "Clearly, we need to keep working on survival training. That part of puppy pirate school will continue long after today. We have a lot of work to do."

All the pups wagged their tails. Wally wasn't the only one who was excited to hear some part of puppy pirate school would carry on!

"Great pirates should always be on the search

for more opportunities to grow and learn," Old Salt barked. "Every day is another chance to learn something new."

"Aye, aye!" Captain Red Beard howled. "But all great pirates know no one can learn on an empty stomach. I be starvin'! Supper, Steak-Eye?"

Steak-Eye barked, "*Aye, aye!*"

So the crew raced to the dining room for dinner. Everyone was very hungry after a busy day of school.

As soon as he had scarfed down his stew, Captain Red Beard barked for attention. "Today's puppy pirate school was filled with exciting new adventures for me crew," he began. "I am proud of each and every one of you for your focus, pirate smarts, and speed. Clearly, I have already done a good job teaching all of you how to be great pirates." He paused, waiting for the crew to cheer for him.

"Three cheers for Captain Red Beard!" the puppies shouted.

Red Beard took a bow. "Thank you. And now the time has come for me to award ribbons to the best pups in school. If you were the winner

during any classes today, please stand up to get your ribbons."

The captain gave Leo, Olly, and the new pup ribbons for mast climbing. He gave Henry and Einstein ribbons for map reading. Millie and Stink—who spent years hiding on a ghost ship—took the prize for hiding class. Piggly was awarded a ribbon for Steak-Eye's cooking class. Marshmallow won top honors in storytelling—his pirate tales were almost as good as Old Salt's!

Curly decided that *no one* should get a ribbon for survival training, since the pups in the dinghy had panicked and put themselves in danger. And, of course, Red Beard gave himself a gold medal for being the best student *and* teacher in captain class. Finally, all the winners had their ribbons.

The new pup looked over at Wally and saw that he didn't have a ribbon. "You can have my ribbon, Wally," she said. "I wouldn't have been one of the best if you hadn't told me your secret tricks to getting up the mast in a hurry."

"You won it, fair and square," Wally told her, pushing the ribbon back to her. "It's yours." He snatched up the last bite of meat in his bowl and tried to feel excited for his friends. He was happy for them but sad for himself.

He realized the only *new* thing puppy pirate school had taught him was that he wasn't the best at anything. Suddenly, school didn't feel so fun after all.

Best Crew on
the Seven Seas

"I think you forgot something," Old Salt said, thumping up to join the captain in front of the crew. "There are a lot of pups who don't yet have their ribbons."

"I didn't forget anyone," the captain said. "Every student who was the best at something got their prize."

"But school isn't about being the *best* at things," Old Salt reminded him. "It's about *learning* things." Old Salt turned to the crew.

"It takes a mighty brave pirate to try learning something new—*especially* if that something new isn't easy for you. How many of you did that today?"

Spike raised his paw. "I learned how to plug up a leaky boat, even though I was scared out of my fur."

Wayne raised his paw. "I learned how to cook a steak!"

Soon puppy after puppy was sticking a paw in the air. Wally looked around. Almost everyone had learned new skills at pirate school. And every time one of his mates howled out something they had learned, Old Salt passed them a ribbon!

"What about you, Wally?" Old Salt asked. "What did you learn at puppy pirate school?"

Wally hung his head. He *really* wanted a ribbon for himself. But he couldn't think of a good answer.

"He already knew plenty about mast climbing!" the new pup yelped. "He taught me all his tricks."

"You helped an old dog like me learn a new trick, too," Old Salt said, telling everyone about how Wally had helped him read a map.

"If Wally hadn't stayed calm during survival training, none of us would have survived!" Spike exclaimed.

Leo agreed. "He acted like a real captain out there."

All the pups started barking at once, talking about how scared they had been.

Old Salt called for attention. "So it seems that you learned something pretty big today, Wally."

Wally cocked his head. "Eh?"

"I think you learned that you know enough about pirating to help your friends," Old Salt said. "Don't you think that deserves a ribbon, Captain?"

Captain Red Beard passed Wally a bright blue ribbon. Wally beamed. He was so used to being the new pup on the ship, he hadn't noticed what a good pirate he had become. Of course he still had a lot to learn. All the pups did. But it felt good to realize how much he already knew. And it felt *extra* good to have a ribbon that proved it.

Wally looked around at the crew, happy to see that everyone had a ribbon now.

"Looks like pirate school was a success, Captain," Curly said.

Captain Red Beard woofed. "Aye, we are now officially the best crew on the seven seas!"

"Yo ho haroo!" barked the new pup. "Three cheers for pirate school! Three cheers for the *Salty Bone!*"

The rest of the crew cheered, "Yo ho haroo!"

"If it hadn't been for you, New Pup, we never would have known about school. Even though you still have much to learn about bein' a great pirate, you have earned your place on board me ship." Captain Red Beard handed the little Lab her pirate bandanna.

The new pup wagged her tail happily and jumped around in circles.

"But," the captain said seriously, "we are going to have to give you a real name now that you're not so new anymore. I need somethin'

to call you when I want to yell at you. So . . .
what's your name gonna be?"

The crew of the *Salty Bone* had learned
how much fun helping each other could be. So
they decided to help the new pup pick a name.
Everyone started barking out suggestions all at
once.

"Stew!" Willard suggested.

"Hidey!" yipped Spike.

"Mike!" howled Puggly.

Then Mille and Stink sang out,

**"You are a Weirdo!
Do you like to dance?
If you're a Weirdo,
your name is . . . Lance!"**

The new pup stood on her back legs and spun in circles, dancing along to the song. Everyone cheered.

Henry was trying to say something, too, but no one could hear him over all the barking and singing. Wally woofed for his friends to be quiet.

"In case you were wondering, there is an important part of school that we forgot," Henry said. "School is hard work, and sometimes you need a break for play. Now that our bellies are full, it's time for . . . recess!"

"Recess!" Captain Red Beard repeated. "That's a good one. Your name, new pup, is Recess."

"Recess!" the new pup said happily. "My very own name! I love it."

Red Beard nodded proudly. "But I might keep callin' you New Pup for a while. The name kinda grew on me."

Wally giggled. Recess was a pretty silly name, but it really did suit the fun, little brown Lab. All the puppy pirates raced up to the deck, ready to celebrate after a day of learning. "Recess!" everyone shouted.

The little pup barked in response, and the whole crew laughed. Wally nosed a ball toward his newest crewmate and barked, "Welcome aboard, Recess!"

Arrr, matey!

Don't stop there—
turn the page for more
Puppy Pirate
fun and adventure!

How to Draw a Treasure Chest!

Follow the steps below to make
your very own treasure chest.

Step 1: Start by drawing a box.

Step 2: Cut the box in half along the middle horizontally. Draw a half circle at the top of the left side of the box. Where the top of the half circle meets the top of the box, draw a line across the top of the box. Draw an arc from this line down to the center line on the front of the box. Add a small square just below the line that cuts the front of the box in half.

Step 3: Erase the lines that outlined the original box. Now you should have a shape that looks more like a treasure chest! Draw lines that are just inside and parallel to the outline of the treasure chest. Don't forget to turn the little square into a lock.

Step 4: Add details such as wood, a keyhole, a handle, and nails. Now you have a treasure chest!

Study Hall Codes

Always pay attention in class! Answer the following questions to put your knowledge of *Best in Class* to the test. You can use a notebook or make a copy of this page if you don't want to write in your book.

1. Piggly and Puggly want Wally to pretend that he is the _ _ _ _ _ _ _.

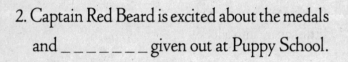

2. Captain Red Beard is excited about the medals and _ _ _ _ _ _ _ given out at Puppy School.

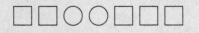

3. In the class on basic skills and obedience, puppies learned about _ _ _ _ _ _ _.

□ □ ○ ○ □ □ □

4. _ _ _ _ _ _ _ dogs are very good at catching and collecting things.

5. On the *Salty Bone,* Olly teaches _ _ _ _ climbing.

◯ ▢ ▢ ◯

6. In Captain Class, Wally's boat falls into the _ _ _ _ _.

◯ ▢ ▢ ◯ ▢

7. The puppy pirates name the new pup _ _ _ _ _ _ .

▢ ▢ ▢ ▢ ◯ ▢

Now look at your answers above. The letters that are circled spell two words—but those words are scrambled! Unscramble the letters to complete the final puzzle.

A brave pirate tries _ _ _ _ _ _ _ _ _ _ _ _ _!

Final Puzzle: A brave pirate tries SOMETHING NEW!

Answers: 1. Captain. 2. Ribbons. 3. Manners. 4. Herding. 5. Mast. 6. Water. 7. Recess.

Pirate School Is in Session!

Recess is going to Pirate School, but her list of classes is all mixed up! Can you help her figure out what time her classes are? Read the clues, then fill in the schedule. Hurry—the bell is about to ring!

- Map Reading class is before Cooking in the Galley but after Captain Class.

- Captain Class is not the first class of the day.

- Mast Climbing comes after Knot Tying.

- Rowing is the first class of the day.

- Cooking in the Galley is before lunch.

- Mast Climbing and Knot Tying are after lunch.

List of Classes	Pirate School Schedule
Mast Climbing	8:00 _____
Map Reading	9:00 _____
Captain Class	10:00 _____
Cooking in the Galley	11:00 _____
Rowing	12:00 LUNCH
Knot Tying	1:00 _____
	2:00 _____

All paws on deck!

Another Puppy Pirates adventure
is on the horizon.
Here's a sneak peek at

Pug vs. Pug

"Anchors aweigh!" barked Captain Red Beard.
"Load our loot into dinghies. Shake the sand off
your fur. It's time for me crew to set sail!"

Puppies of all shapes and sizes raced across a
sandy beach. They shook their bodies, scratched
their ears, and rinsed their paws in salty ocean
water. "Scratch hard, pups! Leave all the bugs here

on shore," Red Beard ordered. Then he chuckled and added, "All the *pugs,* too."

Captain Red Beard's puppy pirate crew had spent the morning searching for buried treasure on a small island in the middle of the sea. They dug up three gold chests filled with tasty bones. Then they celebrated with an afternoon of swimming, chasing, and running. But now it was time to get back to their ship.

"Quickly!" Red Beard barked as pups climbed into the small wooden boats that would return them to their home on the water. "We must get back to the *Salty Bone* at once. The sun is sinking into the sea. When the sun goes underwater, that means night is here."

Wally, a soft golden retriever puppy, cocked his head. "Does the sun *really* go underwater, sir?"

"Aye, aye, *arrrr-oooo!*" Red Beard barked. "I've been a sailor for many years, little Walty. Every night, without fail, the sun plops into the ocean. Then it pops back up on the other side of the world the next morning." The gruff terrier lowered his voice and said, "This here is a fact, pup: the sun hides underwater at night and lights up the deep sea world."

Wally wasn't sure this was true. Sometimes Captain Red Beard mixed up his words and facts. But Wally didn't like to argue with his captain. Wally didn't like to argue with anyone, because it was no fun when other pups were upset with him. He was happiest when everyone got along.

"It's high time we went on our next adventure!" Captain Red Beard said. He jumped into a dinghy just as it set off toward the *Salty Bone*. "Row carefully through these waters," the captain warned his crew. "There are sharp rocks and coral reefs hidden just below the ocean's surface. Keep a close lookout!"

Wally jumped into the last dinghy. Old Salt, a wise peg-legged Bernese mountain dog, was curled up at the front of the little boat. Wally's best mate, a human boy named Henry, hopped in and grabbed the oars.

Henry pointed at the pink-and-gold-streaked sky. "In case you were wondering, mates, a pink sky at night is a sailor's delight. It means good weather is ahead."

"And I've heard a pink sky in the morning means that sailors should take warning," Wally said, "because storms are coming. Is that legend true, Old Salt?"

Old Salt glanced at the pink sky. Then he pointed his paw at a bank of storm clouds gathering on the horizon. "I guess we'll find out, won't we?"

Henry was about to dip the oars into the water and push away from land when Captain Red Beard barked, "Avast!"

Wally's ears pricked. He could hear a worried tone in his captain's voice.

"I forgot something," Red Beard called out. This wasn't a surprise. The captain forgot lots of things. "I sent Curly, Wayne, and the pugs into the woods to gather coconuts. Little Walty, go fetch the last of our crew and help them carry the treats." He nodded toward the trees.

"Aye, aye, Captain," Wally barked back. He jumped out of the dinghy and raced across the sand.

Henry chased after him, calling, "Wait up, mate. Wait for me!"

"Better hustle, little Walty!" the captain howled from way offshore. He squinted at the sun, which was sinking into the sea. "The sun is almost all wet, and the waters around this island are too rocky to row through after dark!"

Wally and Henry ran as fast as their legs could go. The jungle forest was bright and cheerful during the day. But now that it was getting dark, Wally noticed that the trees cast spooky shadows.

Not far off, Wally could hear the pug sisters yipping at each other. He zipped through the brush and burst into a clearing. The grassy, open space was lined with beautiful palm trees that hung heavy with coconuts. Wally had tasted coconut a few times before. The meat was sweet and creamy, but the outside had funny little hairs that tickled his lips. Wally knew never to eat too much coconut, because that meant tummy trouble.

On one side of the clearing, Curly and Wayne were working together. Curly was the *Salty Bone*'s first mate. Wayne the Great Dane was the biggest pup on their crew. Curly and Wayne made a perfect coconut-picking team. When Curly stood on Wayne's back, she could reach the lowest coconuts on the trees. The pair had filled nearly four rolling crates to bring back to their ship.

Piggly and Puggly hadn't filled a single crate. Instead, the pugs had found a way to make mischief. "Wally!" Piggly yelped. "Want to try our coconut collector?"

"Look, they made a trampoline!" Henry exclaimed. Using ropes twisted around a cluster of springy branches, the two little pugs had created a bouncy platform. They were taking turns jumping high into the air.

"It's time to get back to the ship," Wally barked to his crewmates. "Captain says we have to hurry!" Curly and Wayne howled to show they had heard him. But the pugs were yapping too loudly to hear the orders.

Piggly soared into the air, snagged a coconut, and tossed it to the ground. Then Puggly took her turn. They jumped and tossed, over and over again. Coconuts rolled across the ground. Piggly announced that she could jump the highest. Puggly yipped that she could toss the farthest. Piggly said she was best at breaking the coconuts when she tossed them. Puggly claimed she was best at hitting a target.

"Hey, pugs!" Wally shouted. The trees' shadows were growing longer and darker by the minute. "We really need to go or we'll be stranded!"

"One last jump," Piggly snorted. She barked to her sister, "Me, then you."

At the same time, Puggly howled, "Me, then you!"

The two pugs jumped high into the air together. They crashed into each other. They thrashed. They snarled. And then they fell.

Down.

Down.

Down.

Ker-plop! The two chubby pugs tumbled into Curly and Wayne's crates, sending hundreds of furry fruits flying.

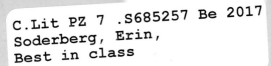

New friends. New adventures.
Find a new series . . . just for you!

BALLPARK *Mysteries*

FOR THE SPORTS FAN

THE DINO FILES

FOR THE ADVENTURER

Louise Trapeze

FOR THE SUPERSTAR

PIPER GREEN

FOR THE DREAMER

PUPPY PIRATES

FOR THE ANIMAL LOVER

Totally True adventures!

FOR THE EXPLORER

Illustrations (from left to right) : © Mark Meyers; © Mike Boldt; © Brigette Barrager; © Qin Leng; © Russ Cox; © Wesley Lowe

RandomHouseKids.com

1220